Advance Praise for

"With two writers as well matched artistically as Tara Lynn Masih and James Claffey, a collaboration is cause to celebrate. This richly woven, haunting novelette transcends the confines of its brevity; feels tender, sprawling, immersive. *The Bitter Kind* is an alchemy, a duet, a gorgeous melding of two of our most treasured literary voices."
—Kathy Fish, author of *Wild Life: Collected Works from 2003–2018*

"With short, alternating passages, James Claffey and Tara Masih vividly illuminate the separate and commingled lives of Stela and Brandy in this original and elegantly textured novella. It is a story, human and soulful, of place, mysticism, and the hard-won ground we all struggle toward."
—Robert Scotellaro, author of *Nothing Is Ever One Thing*

"From ghost-soaked frontier towns to leafy waterways, frozen river basins, and the open road, Tara Masih's and James Claffey's parallel narratives tumble along through stunning landscapes of loneliness and beauty. The writing is evocative and tender, exploring both the haunted and the haunting; touching in its examination of broken things and masterful in its prose."
—Kimberly Lojewski, author of *Worm Fiddling Nocturne in the Key of a Broken Heart*

"With beautiful imagery and a seamless voice, Masih and Claffey move us through decades as two parallel lives seek solace and healthy human connection. Stela, long plagued by abusive relationships, and Brandy, spurred by tragedy and unlucky in love, are shaped and steered by the things that haunt them, and, perhaps, the things that will someday guide them to heal. This winning collaborative effort is both stirring and satisfying."
—Mel Bosworth, author of *FREIGHT* and coauthor of *Second Acts in American Lives*

"With their binocular lyric lenses, Masih and Claffey provide a lacquered and sanded depth to this compilation set in the chambered karst of our heartfelt heartland. The book is a layered lanyard, a laurel wreath, an ouroboros, Mobius's Mobius, an

effortless *enso*, and a terrific torqueing torus. The diastolic/systolic dub-Dub, a syncopated sink or swim, of the call and response had me reeling, a time step timed to hit the one and the three. What I am saying is that this is a *tour de force*, a *fait accompli*."
—Michael Martone, author of *Brooding* and *The Moon Over Wapakoneta*

The Bitter Kind

A Flash Novelette

Tara Lynn Masih
&
James Claffey

Červená Barva Press
Somerville, Massachusetts

Červená Barva Press
P.O. Box 440357
W. Somerville, MA 02144-3222

www.cervenabarvapress.com

Bookstore: www.thelostbookshelf.com

Cover Photo: Ashley Inguanta

Cover Design: Sophie Appel

ISBN: 978-1-950063-40-6

Dedicated to our supportive spouses,
Maureen Foley and Michael Gilligan

The Bitter Kind

Part I

1942–1982

Stela

Stela's father was a ship's Captain, a drinker, a wanderer of
the world, always at sea, exotic port cities, a career suited to
the assiduous lifestyle of the hardened drinker. At home in
Alabama, in their old-fashioned colonial house one month
out of every six, he'd roar at her mother and send Stela
running for the safety of her bedroom. Her brother sat in the
corner of his room, two years younger than Stela, and
covered his ears with his hands. The Tuscaloosa house was an
anomaly for the area; red-bricked, ivy-covered walls and roses
and begonias in the garden. Her mother spent hours pruning
and digging in the soil, a practice that kept her only just this
side of sanity. The walls of the house were covered with old
wheels from steamer ships, brass lights from ferries, and huge
knots from God knows where. He kept the whiskey in the
brass lamp inside the door, hidden by the accumulated years
of dust. Nobody was allowed to touch the lamp, and once,
when her mother had polished it to a brilliant shine and
dusted the glass from the inside, too, the Captain had
clattered Stela's mother on the head with the back of his
hand.

Times he'd be lovely, though. Saturdays, when he was
at home, he'd take her mother dancing at the local Legion
hall, and in his dress blues he looked so handsome. All the
other wives *oohed* and *aahed* over the Captain, according to her
mom, who always wore her Chanel two-piece and dabbed
some mysterious perfume behind each ear, and on the inside
of each wrist. Those nights, good humor filled the house and
both parents climbed the stairs to bed, giving the illusion of
being the happiest of married couples. Once, her mother
showed to breakfast with a bruised cheekbone, but she said it
had happened when she bent down to take her tights off in
the bathroom and caught her face on the sink.

Stela dreamed of being eighteen so she could leave the house and make a life for herself. The fact she'd have to leave both brother and mother with the Captain saddened her. In the dark of her bedroom, her secret world unfolded. There, she made attempts to figure out what exactly was going on in the house during those nights when the Captain steered to shore and laid a soft hand on her cheek, whispering to her in the dark. A sea shanty sung damage and Stela bore the blows in silence. Instead of sails on a yacht, she felt the bottoms of the family coats rustle in the interminable blackness. "Say a word to anyone and I'll dig a hole and bury you in it," he said, hands about her arms, his raspy sour breath on her face. "Nobody would believe you," he went on. His reputation was unimpeachable.

She tried to avoid the Captain, creeping out of the house in the mornings before he awoke, always hopeful he might not visit her in the night and turn her face to the wall as if trying to avoid her gaze. Worry became Stela's closest friend in those early teenage years. One day while the Captain was out in the yard shoveling leaves into burlap sacks, she considered staving his head in with the heavy shovel on the grass beside him. Her piety, the constant prayer meetings in the narrow Baptist Church on Elm Lane, and her fear, stayed her. To spill his blood into the dry Alabama soil, to cover his body with sticks and debris, to free herself from his torture. If the Captain died, she'd not shed a tear. Not a one. Maybe there'd be a treasure chest under her parents' bed she could pillage and take to the open road in the rusting old Chevy pickup? Instead, Stela knew she was almost her father's pet, a leashed creature to be kept subservient. Her mother, bless her, was timid to the point of muteness, and wouldn't be any help to Stela in the war against the Captain. Stela wanted to slide into a deep sleep, one from which she could not awaken. Even the Captain would be powerless to do anything to her if she couldn't respond to his groping hands.

Sting in the tail, her fragile body covered by a carapace of resolve, Stela circles the washrag around the kitchen counter, the lemon peel and almond bits collecting in a mound. "'Tis the season to be jolly," she sings, her voice low, so as not to awaken her father. He swung back into town from a three-month haul down to Argentina with a shipment of lumber. Her mother shrinks when the Captain returns to dry land and her brother disappears for days, preferring to spend the holidays with his school friends. When the Captain is away there's an expansion that takes place in her, as if she's coming out of a tight hiding space and retaking her original shape. After months in a cabin, the Captain declares himself to be sick and tired of the ocean blue, and resolves to land a desk job with the shipping company and move the entire family the two-hundred miles from Tuscaloosa, with Stela's beloved Black Warrior River and water oaks, to Mobile, where he can throw his feet on his desk and drink gin morning to night. He's a handy man with the bottle, Stela thinks, dreading the thought of leaving behind the leafy waterways for the bleak expanse of the Gulf Coast. "God, no. I don't want to leave here," she says, rolling her eyes at her father as he plumps her cheek with his thumb and forefinger. "It's my paychecks that put food on the table and clothes on your back," he replies, "so you'll do my bidding." Her mother, pale and quiet in the kitchen, says little, only how they'll have to adapt to the humidity of the Gulf and all its swarms of flying cockroaches.

Her passion is music. American. Gershwin. Antheil. Copland. The Victrola sits in the family room, next to the large potted hibiscus. She sits on the Captain's lap, the swell of the music and the tapping of his feet on the carpet. His nose is straight and sharp, and in profile he reminds her of those faces on Roman coins. Her Emperor. Her captor. His act at church when the pastor greets the family, and the backslapping manner of the Captain, makes her want to throw up. She thinks this will go on forever, season-to-season, the way magnolia blossoms come and go. On New Year's Eve her parents toast the future decade and clink crystal glasses together in the downstairs dining room. "To the future! Down the hatch!" She hears their toasts.

Stela tosses and turns in bed like the restless sea as the strains of "Auld Lang Syne" filter up through the floorboards.

"A cheap hussy," is what the Captain calls her when Stela goes to a school dance dressed in a blue-and-white striped dress and red cowboy boots. Since moving to Mobile she has put on weight. Her mother puts it down to the fried food. Now she is plump, her teenage body no longer gangly and awkward. She has curves and the Captain's nightly visits increase. A dollop of gin and he's a dangerous man. Stela takes her medicine, biding her time. Her mother folds egg whites into sugar for meringues and the Captain grills steak, medium; ears of corn and sinewy beef, his favorite food in the humid summertime. Sometimes he drives to the butcher's shop and buys slabs of meat off the hook. He brought a set of horns home the last time and fastened them to the front of the Chevy, prompting Stela to mutter something about any more bull in the family and she'd kill herself. That led to a near injury when she drove the truck straight at the Captain and nearly gored him.

About their house, collected trucks and cars rust and fall asunder as her father keeps accumulating them at nearby auctions. He particularly likes the trucks—old Chevys and Fords—and their beaten-up exteriors, scars to the work they'd put in over the years. It was, she thought, his one soft spot when it came to revealing his true self. Too often he railed at her and her mother, the liquor igniting his practically nonexistent fuse. But when it came to the vehicles that graveyarded their property, the *junkyard*, as her mother called it behind his back, well, they received most of his attention, the positive attention, that is. Stela remembers tying her hair ribbons on the fenders of her favorites, and how the Captain always smiled at her when she wrapped a yellow sash on one of the trucks. "Good eye for a vehicle," he said, frequently. An ear for music, too, which was why she spent so much time in her bedroom in front of the mirror crooning into her hairbrush, seeing, instead of her awkward teenage self, the curvy shape of Connie Francis. How well proportioned she was, compared to, say, Stela's mom, whose behind was playfully named "the caboose" by the Captain. A taste for buttery food was to blame; the kitchen a constant source of baked goods like angel cakes and apple pies. "Goddamned piggy eyes," he said, as he caught Stela choosing her favorite angel cake, her eyes scrunched to see which one contained the most cream.

Brandy

It is spring, during the Great Depression, when their neighbor Al Close finally finds the Ghost Wolf that has been haunting every cattle rancher and sheep herder's farm from the Highwood Mountains to the Little Belts. More than 1,800 cattle and sheep lost to the vicious hunter who melts in and out of the night like a banshee ghost and takes its victims down in its strong jaws, sometimes leaving them partly alive as it flees to its hiding place.

Al's red Irish terrier and sheep dog track it down, finally, though no one on horseback or looking out of an airplane has been able to find this menace. His dogs, trained for this moment, know what to do. They break into the sleeping wolf's dreams, as it lies curled in the underbrush, and the terrier latches on to its tail and the sheep dog flushes it out so that Al can admire the huge beast in the moonlight, this larger than life wolf whose white fur glows like a fallen star. Just before Al pulls the trigger, he feels a spark of regret.

This is the story Brandy grows up hearing on his birthday, because this momentous thing happened on the night he was born.

"You got some of that spirit wolf in you," his Cree mother likes to say. "It left that divine animal and entered you, that's why you so stubborn."

His mother is Judith, named after the mountains she fled to with her white trapper husband. They left the basin valley full of cross-breed Chippewas to find gold and sapphires in the rough but accessible lands above. They found little, just small pieces and stones in streams, enough to lay claim to a few acres. Eventually Brandy's father, Jake Crawford, had to go back to what he knew—hunting and logging.

Judith is famous for her pemmican. Brandy often stands by her side, watching her grind the dry buffalo or deer meat, and fry the fat. She lets him mix in berries and form the cakes of rich protein for local hunters and Indians who make their difficult way across country.

Brandy doesn't know who he is. Indian? White? Wolf? He howls at his mother sometimes, and she throws him bits of jerky in response. He catches them in his mouth and chews, then runs out the door into the patchwork sunlight and onto the humus carpet on all fours.

Brandy's father is not around much during the lean years. He is off cutting down lodgepole pine or trapping wolves for the farmers. He gets enough money from both to get his family out of the dark hillside dugout and into a one-story cabin made of cottonwood and spackled with clay. This was his promise to his young Cree bride, that one day she would have a home in the mountains that mirrored the ones in the Judith Basin. For days she scraped calf skins, which Jake had bartered for with his last trapped wolf, till they were translucent enough to serve as windows.

Brandy stands on a wood crate and peers at the world for the first time through a square space. For hours, he sometimes stands. Watching the light outside move from east to west, the blur of birds fly by, the shaking of aspen leaves glitter like round spheres in the sun. It is all so beautiful and new to him.

His school is the Bible. Judith makes him read to her every day. Her Chippewa ancestors had converted to Catholicism when they married the French colonizers, making them even more separate from other Indians. She wears black dresses, like her mother and sisters, and had given up her colorful tartan shawl for a black one when she married. She is a Landless Indian. That means she has cause to resent the government that will not recognize her people nor grant them the land they settled.

She is an angry woman, too, most of the time. All her movements reveal her disquietude, from walking with emphasis on the bare wood floor, to pounding the pemmican, to bathing him with rough hands. Brandy thinks love is rough and hurts sometimes. Even his large, bearded father, when he comes home now and then, hits him hard on the back as a hello.

When Brandy is old enough to know he is not a wolf, he walks about only on two feet, exploring the mountainside and streams. This is where he is touched more gently. By cold, rippling currents and shifting, fluttering new leaves. He raises a baby rabbit that curls against him when he sleeps, its slippery soft tail tickling his side. He loves the feathery presence that means something needs his protection.

When his head reaches the top of his father's belt, he is taken into the woods to mark the property lines for the lumber company. His father carries a brush-ax to clear the undergrowth that covers the borders. Someone else carries a flat iron tool to scrape the bark from the trees, and Brandy carries a bucket of sky-blue paint and a brush to mark two horizontal stripes on the tree to show which trees are on the inside of the property, and to mark one horizontal stripe to show which trees grow outside.

Sometimes, when the men aren't looking, he will leave only one stripe on a tree that looks especially ancient, hoping no one will notice it actually sits inside the now jagged property line.

The men call the tree forest "gold on a stump." But Brandy can hear the trees crying and moaning. They aren't dead like gold. They live. Sometimes, the moans are covered by the sounds of nearby waterfalls and small rivers spilling over mountain rocks. But there are days, especially when the mist still clings to the mountains and they work above the line, and his father swings his brush-ax, that Brandy has to squint from the painful cries echoing in his ears, and in the particles of damp air that slowly warm around them.

The mountain fever comes to both his parents. He watches helplessly as they roll around in their bed, hot and vomiting into the covers, bright red splotches flowering on their wrists and spreading up their arms.

He tries to stop the red from spreading. He takes cold cloths and dips them into the cool creek that runs by the home. He wraps their arms and thighs, listens to their rantings. Only once do his mother's eyes clear to recognition, and she strokes his hair before the fever takes her again. He will never know if it was emotion or weakness that made her touch gentle for the first time.

He runs barefoot through the woods to the Close farm, but nothing can be done.

They bury Jake in the same hole as Judith, on the side of the mountain named after her. It is summer and buck brush is blooming. Brandy breaks off some of the pink flowers and sprinkles them like sugar on the dark black mound. It reminds him of berries in pemmican. For the first time he cries, thinking of his mother—her roughness, her stories, her song. Her angry love. Her belief in his spirit.

They take him back down from the mountain, back down to the high basin. He is surrounded by black. Black dresses, black hats, black shawls. He can see the Judith Mountains in the east. He knows the Ghost Wolf has wandered through the entire range, from the Little Belts, to the Snowy Mountains, to the Highwoods. He tries to feel like he has come home.

Stela

At Auburn University, Stela dates a radio enthusiast from Wisconsin, and an economics major from Idaho (with the nickname of Boise). Either of them would happily march her down the aisle, but she prefers Boise, yet craves independence and her own money. She lightens her hair at a salon in town, and when the hairdresser finishes she shakes her corn-yellow hair and laughs at the stranger in the mirror with the same smile and the same eyes as hers. Her own father won't recognize her, she thinks, and hands over the cash to the stylist.

In the winter, snow on the ground. Boise invites her to his parents' for Thanksgiving and she phones her mother to tell her she won't be home for the holidays. Stela knows the Captain will want her there, but she knows he'll come to her room when the house is quiet and put his hand over her mouth again.

Over a lunch of celery and mayo sandwiches, Boise says his plans have changed. A girl from St. Charles, Louisiana, has stolen his heart, and he'd not known how to tell Stela. She tries to reason with him, to talk him out of leaving, but it's too late, he tells her.

Stela takes to her bed and howls into her pillow for a week. When she comes to, embittered and hating all to do with Idaho, her butt looks to have gotten smaller; a pyrrhic victory. The next boy to tangle with her emotions, well, he'll see what she's made of. Instead of attending dances as usual, Stela stays in weekends and studies, cursing the Hairball from Boise who's crushed her heart. She slumps over her desk, writing bad poetry for weeks, harping on about Boise's callousness without actually speaking of the breakup. Eventually, with the snow melting and spring on the way, she drags herself to the student union for a dance with a couple of friends who think it'd be a fine remedy for her low spirits. But it's not, and she knows her heart is still fragile, a tender snowdrop on a narrow green shoot that might snap in the wind at any given moment.

Spring semester consists of elaborate schemes to avoid running into Boise, who she's unfortunately come upon in the line at the local Waffle House with his new girl. Stela can't believe she's been dumped for a mousy-looking girl with a thin upper lip, too much mascara, eyeliner, and stringy brown hair.

Stela hates makeup and the way it leaves her skin pitted like a bad piece of meat. She is what her mother terms a "natural beauty," gifted with clear skin and bright eyes. Her mother routinely examines her daughter's profile whenever she arrives home from school, running her eyes from top to toe, calculating the added pounds or excess flab she might be carrying. Probably she is worried Stela will continue to follow in the family tradition of big behinds and wants to spare her the burden.

Stela feels her mother's judgment, the pity in her stare, after Boise breaks her heart. She vows to take up running around the pond adjacent to the football stadium. She takes to the frozen streets of their town and jogs her sadness to death. Feels better, for sure. Better than stuffing her mom's cakes and pies into her mouth and adding pounds atop the guilt.

Stela returns home for a short visit at Easter. Her mother tells her on the phone that the Captain is delayed at a car auction in Montgomery. In her room, she plucks at her eyebrows, and at one stage she pretty much removes both her brows. Her routine is the same as the kids' game played with daisies, "He loves me, he loves me not." She makes sure to end on "He loves me," though she knows this to not be true.

After the shock of seeing her eyebrows gone, she pencils them back on and drags a small amount of grease over the raw flesh with her index finger to ease the itch. To add insult to her bitterness, she singes her hair with the curling iron right before Easter Mass, and has to wear a bright yellow bandeau to hide the burn. She doesn't linger outside the church, citing a headache, which, in fact, is true. When she arrives back at the house, she rests her head on the arm of the sofa in her bedroom and stares into the lights of the lava lamp until she falls asleep.

In the dream, the Captain wears his full-dress uniform with the shining buttons and the tassels on his shoulders. She can smell the gin on his breath, and the bay rum he splashes into his cupped hands and runs through his hair, combing the strands back tightly. Instead of unzipping his trousers and pinning her to the bed like he usually does, this time he opens his mouth wide and swallows her whole, headfirst. Stela wakes in a sweat, the terror of the Captain's love still there in the air, his faint scent in the dark room.

By the time she's ready to go back to school, her mother signs on at the local community college for a ceramics class, and Stela, with the Captain at auction, is light and trouble-free. On the last night, she climbs out the window of her room, scales the fire ladder to the roof, and lies on the slates, staring into the vast velvet cloth of the universe, the pinpricks of light reminding her that other loves await.

She meets him at the drugstore, his broad chest rippling beneath a Lynyrd Skynyrd tank top. Inside, couples sip from shared malts and shakes, plates of crispy French fries and little tubs of ketchup between them. She's with Karen, smoking, when he approaches, two beers in his hands. He raises an eyebrow and says, "Evening, ladies." They both smile, but nothing more.

"Y'all are college girls?"

"Sure are. This here's Karen, and I'm Stela."

"Burdine. Nice to meet you ladies." He hangs about the exit, joining them when Stela points a hand at an empty chair. Karen beams at him, her straight white teeth movie star bright, but the guy eyes Stela like a cat about to eat a fish. He looks dopey, she thinks, but nice, yes, nice. His hair is black and curly, tight coils like springs. His twang gives Stela goose bumps and she reddens as he stares into her eyes and asks, "You ladies like the rodeo?"

Five minutes later they're in his Camaro heading for the highway. Karen and Stela both wear denim shorts, too-short shorts. Karen's hair flies across her face with the breeze coming in the open windows, and Stela pulls hers into a tight ponytail. Burdine, Stela can tell, is eyeing both girls as he steers one-handed onto the two-lane highway. He pulls a flask from the glove compartment and offers it back to them. Karen waves him off, but Stela takes the flask and swallows a mouthful of the burning liquid. The car smells of bacon and earwax, she thinks, wondering if he has a brain or not, wondering if his devilishly handsome secret is picking his ears whilst cruising along looking for pretty girls. She knows it's impolite to form an opinion about someone based on first impressions, but she can't help see Burdine as a bit of a hick.

"So, where you from?" she asks.

"Louisiana." He takes another pull on the neck of the flask, wipes his mouth with his sleeve and smiles.

"Big country, right," Stela says.

"Yes Ma'am. Timber, that's what my family grows." Stela wants to see the forested land, the spread sky with white clouds scudding the blue.

At the rodeo they buy bacon burgers and Budweiser longnecks, walk the perimeter and check out the bulls in their narrow, fenced cages. One cage has a label stuck on the front that says, "Renew your faith. Pray to Jesus." Burdine laughs, removes it from the metal barrier and crumples it in his fist.

They sit at the top of the small grandstand on the long planks that serve as seating. Through steer wrestling, horse races, and the gimpy clowns who come in to distract the bulls when a rider falls, the girls have a fine time, and when it's all over Burdine delivers them to their dorm room and makes certain to get the phone number, promising to take them out again real soon.

Stela orders sweet pickles with her burger the night Burdine finally takes her to a quiet hotel on the outside of town. "VACANCY" flashing neon and the eternal flask of bourbon promise her the night of her life. She's seduced by the way his eyebrows raise independently when she asks him a question he doesn't know the answer to; like the time she wonders if he's ever thought of visiting Europe. "Jesus Christ, why in God's good name would I leave this fine and proper country?" He seems disturbed by her question, the intimation that there might be a civilization better than theirs out there too much to consider.

When she buries her face in his neck at the bar she detects the familiar scent of bay rum in his hair and can't get the picture of the Captain out of her mind. Burdine kisses her roughly and says they should be getting back to the hotel, as he's tired from his day's work.

She goes quiet and walks back to the room in her bare feet. Her soles tickle in the short cut grass and her giggles break the awkward silence that has descended between them. Shared mouthfuls of the bitter liquor lead to the bed, the springs squeaking beneath their weight. Burdine's hair is greasy from lack of washing and Stela leads him to the shower, where she soaps him down and massages his scalp to the rhythm of moths fizzling dead on the outside light bulb. She tries to wash the bay rum away, but no matter how much she rinses his hair, the scent lingers.

She feels his fist grab her hair and he maneuvers her back to the bed, where his hands pin her down and his mouth opens to hers. The wrap gives way and in the dimness they make hard love as a warm wind blows through the screen door.

On the wall beside the door is a bright green flyswatter, and Stela imagines Burdine tapping her behind with it. What a dumbass I am, she thinks, knowing her lover to be more of a gentleman than that. As he comes, his entire weight crushes her into the mattress and she closes her eyes and dreams of cake; a yellow vanilla one with hummingbirds iced all around it. The next morning, he pays the bill with cash and Stela stows the flyswatter in her bag. Back on the highway, Burdine cranks the engine and speeds back toward town. By the time they pull up outside her place, she wants to get inside and wash the memory of bay rum off her skin. Burdine grins, winking at her, and says, "See you later, pretty lady."

They marry in the fall as swallows, then bats, swarm the air outside the small chapel with the wonderful round, stained-glass window she loves so much. Burdine is more handsome than ever in his immaculate tuxedo, his hair swept back across his forehead, his eyes hoarse with crying for love of Stela. Her parents and brother sit in the front pew, the Captain's face painted regretful. Her mother stares at her feet, afraid to say a word. Stela expects the Captain not to walk her down the aisle, and she is right, even though her brother tries to intervene and persuade him otherwise. Her heart shrinks. She understands the disappointment she's visited on her family, by marrying a man from the backwoods of Louisiana, will perhaps last a lifetime. Burdine's parents, on the other hand, are thrilled that their boy has come good and married a college girl with a "head on her shoulders," as his father puts it at their wedding rehearsal at the BBQ Shack.

All her regretful feelings and panic fade as the band strikes up in the church hall. They dance for hours, stopping only to answer the *tink* of glass when one relative or another calls for a toast, which involves the bride and groom kissing until the tinkling stops. Stela's father gives a brief speech about loyalty, respect, and honor, causing her to blush deeply. Her mother sips on her Chardonnay. Her brother is too taken by some of her college friends to care much at all. Stela dreams of soft cotton sheets and big fires on winter nights. What she does not dream of is the long-sleeved dress she'll wear for years to hide the bruises Burdine layers on her body for the three years of their marriage.

Barren. He calls her barren and breaks her spirit with his iron muscles and scented hair, pinning her to the mattress and willing conception. College friends sometimes call on the phone and he tells them she's gone to town with her new friends. Soon the phone no longer rings. Stela keeps a tidy house and cooks the way he wants her to. Everything she does is to placate his rage. He buys her jewelry, turquoise bangles and rings, and pledges to change. She calls him *thief* and *heretic* as he breaks her body and spirit.

She fantasizes about one of the cowboys from the rodeo that time she first met Burdine. How she begs to be kidnapped by the thick-torsoed man with the wide Stetson and shiny belt buckle. She dreams of darning his socks by an oil lamp on their ranch in Wyoming, but knows the rodeo left town long ago and that now her only escape is in the stories she listens to on the radio in the evenings.

The night he comes to her with a brick in his hand and says she needs to cook his hamburger through so the meat isn't pink no more, is the night she decides to run away. In the dark of the bedroom, her fingers trace the lump on her head from where he thumped her. He did it in silence. Even the Captain would sometimes mutter to her about loving her so much, and how he wished he were stronger. Burdine beat his worry into her body, as she lay defenseless as a spring lamb beneath him: different, but familiar.

As the mosquito buzzes about her head, Burdine snores, the brick still in his hand.

Stela takes to the road the weekend Burdine goes fishing with his high school buddies; a cooler of beer and a half-rack of smoked venison to tide them over as they await their haul. Burdine fastens bait to hooks, and Stela folds her few good pieces of clothing into the narrow suitcase she took on her honeymoon. Burdine and his buds holler and clink bottles, whilst Stela sits on the side of the road, waiting to thumb a lift into a future she knows shall hold no more bruises and no more beatings.

Brandy

While the Basin is well-watered and rich in birds, game, and wildflowers, it is still flat land. Brandy has to adjust to always having the dirt-glazed soles of his feet on the same even plain. Slowly, he gets used to gazing toward what he used to know—the rocky, brush-covered face of a terrain that requires more thought to walk and live on.

But there is more human life down below, more heartache and beatings and death, set amongst the one-story, gaudy-painted houses fashioned from local cottonwood.

There is more celebration, too. Activity and music. Uncle Joseph plays the fiddle during festivals, and Brandy struggles to learn the Red River jig. He dances around the bonfires, mimicking his French ancestors' foot lifts and twirls. He wants to fit in. He is so far away from his wolf past now. No longer feels the Ghost Wolf is following him. Its oversized foot pads, which make no sound when they fall, no longer leave impressions in the new spring snow.

It is a warm winter when Brandy chooses to leave the Basin. Dandelions and clover heads worm their way up through hard earth, answering the call of the warming sun. The flower heads shiver their solitude in the wind, however; the bees are still in hibernation.

He gets hard slaps on the back from his uncles, and a kiss on each cheek from the aunt who'd raised him as best she could.

"Keep an eye out for the snowbirds," she says. "If they flock, you will know a snow storm is coming." He knows this snowbird legend that can save a man's life, has heard it many times before winter hunts, but he nods as if she is giving him something new and important, squeezes both her hands.

His young cousin gifts him a dreamcatcher she made of tender twigs and bright feathers. "To keep away the nightmares when your family isn't around." He pats the top of her auburn head awkwardly and pushes the protective circle into his rucksack with care.

When a tribal member leaves the Basin, the whole village gathers to watch. They stand like somber sentinels as Brandy breaks away from their rutted dirt roads and harsh lives. He crosses a dry meadow, heading toward Helena to find work building cabins or hotels. The East has been encroaching on Montana, and business is booming in the larger towns. Not in the Cree Basin, where time seems to have stopped as his people wait to be recognized.

Tall grass and sagebrush and islands of lodgepole pine obstruct his path to the Missouri River. Once there, the brush opens up and he can walk more freely. He follows the riverbanks, looking for a safe place to cross. There is still blue-white ice clutching river rocks and weeds, but he finds a low-lying curve where the spring flow from the mountains above is not high yet and is crossable.

Before he puts his boots into the rushing water, he looks back. The Ghost Wolf entered his campsite last night. He'd woken to find its large paw prints circling the fire and his sleeping form. He knew it was his wolf because the pads were larger, and one claw was missing, torn off while escaping one of the many traps it had eluded in life.

He stands now, listening to the grasses whisper, looking for shadows, even though he knows he will not see it during the day. Might not see it again. Would it cross the river? He does not know.

"Good-bye, old friend," he speaks loudly, hoping his voice will carry across the divide between two parallel lives.

After several weeks he arrives at the town, looking like most men who come down from or across the Big Belt Mountain range—disheveled, bearded, tattered from branches and nettles, haggard and quiet from being alone for too long

"Ask for John Quigley up at Frontier Town," a trapper he had run into on the other side of the river had told him. "It's west of Helena, and east of the McDonald Pass. When you get close you'll hear the machine voice of a dog barking. It's one of his new exhibits at the entrance. Place is booming and they always need someone handy with a hammer."

Brandy had shared a dried apple with the man as thanks, and moved on. After some consideration, he decided he liked the idea of working a steady job for one boss. So he skirted Helena and kept heading west.

He hears it, faint at first. But he heads toward the sound. It grows into the recognized form of a dog barking in warning. Stopping. Repeating. The same intonations. Over and over the barks echo through the hills.

It becomes part of the daily background, the dog's barking. He learns to tune it out as countless tourists push the button to start the mechanized grizzly attack against the lumberjack and dog. They can't get enough of the mechanical man in flannel who raises his ax and the dog who lunges forward, protecting its master. Over and over. Occasionally it breaks down and the town's mechanic fixes it. It makes too much money in quarters to let it go still for too long.

When Brandy had first seen it, he'd hesitated, not used to such fakery and never having seen a machine made for something besides farming, logging, or mining. This served no working purpose. Because he'd arrived in early summer, he stood in the hot sun. Not moving forward, wary of what lay ahead. But he had no choice. He had to continue up the hill to the pioneer log town. At the summit, he walked up to a gate squared off by four blockhouses. Before he passed through, he took note of the fact that it was a fake fortress built to keep out his fellow ancestors.

His gaze then shifted to the site of a small admissions booth to the left of the gate, housing two pretty women handing out copper $1 tokens.

Brandy gets the job immediately, and works his way through several of the young admissions girls. Until the day that Elizabeth arrives, shiny and lively, fresh off the local stage in Helena. Something gives in him, and he marries her in the tourist chapel overlooking the Great Rocky Mountains. A cross floats in the front window glass, as if hung from invisible threads from the heavens. Brandy hopes this is a sign of his mother's approval.

He stands apart at his own reception, down in the underground frontier bar. He is usually more comfortable away from crowds, and this is a big one. All forty employees, the boss, and the boss's wife, Susan.

Elizabeth is flirting with all the lonely, single men in this fake pioneer town of logs held together by wooden pegs. Her leg is exposed and glistening bright white from the silk stockings she'd borrowed from a theater friend, and the black garter that holds them up peeks out from beneath the white peasant dress of ruffles and eyelet.

Topped by a crown of wilted daisies, her glorious curls rain down, brushing the tops of the crew-cut heads. He's discussed the color with her countless times and they can't agree whether it's gold or copper. It changes.

She's sitting on the longest bar top in Montana, the pride and joy of his boss's making. Maybe even the longest bar in the United States. A 50-foot-long split Douglas fir log, etched with Western scenes, covered by protective glass. The men toss back beers, and she leans in and sips from a few mugs. When she lifts her head to reveal a frothy beer mustache, she laughs, casually brushing it with the back of her hand, the hand that now holds the simple wedding band he'd managed to purchase down in Helena.

Behind her, Old West mechanical dioramas move when someone deposits a quarter. He leans against the far end of the shiny, melon-hued bar, talking with half an ear to a friend. The tinfoil eagle soars a few feet, the fisherman's wire goes taut, and the little flashes of yellow electricity burst from miniature guns in a mock Indian–Cowboy war.

He wonders what part of this diorama he would fit into. There is no wolf in the scene.

After the customers have gone home, and the town is shut down, John Quigley shoots a black bear right in that same bar that very night. Its powerful paws had ripped through the corrugated metal siding that lay next to the food supply for the bar restaurant.

The bear is stuffed and put on display. "Killed Where You Stand," reads the carved plaque. Brandy stares into its brown glass eyes with an apology.

She always has a reason, when he asks, to not have a child. And repeats the reasons right after sex, when his whole body is thrumming with pleasure and her fiery hair envelops him. He shuts his eyes to her excuses.

She avoids holding his hand now when they walk through the log town in the evenings to get beer or a soda pop. He does not reach for her hand anymore. It is a loss that he feels deep in his center.

He feels important when he is asked to help Mr. Quigley get his Bear Vision display up and running. Shooting the black bear that had come in from the woods had inspired his boss.

"I don't know what to tell you," his boss, married almost thirty years, says as they work at a large stump with a 12-foot circumference. They decide they need a tractor to drag the stumps to the viewing area, where the closed-circuit monitor will be rigged up for bargoers to watch the bear feed on top of the stumps.

"I just keep moving forward. I got so many ideas in this ol' head of mine, they just never stop coming. My good wife, she just works to keep up. And somehow she does. And I appreciate the gal to death. And I let her know it every chance I get.

"I don't know what advice to give, since I was gifted with this woman. I'm a Catholic, so're you. But I don't put calluses on my knees with my prayer, I put 'em on my hands. This all"—he waves at the huge stumps, the log town looming behind them—"this is my prayer. Maybe you're the same."

Brandy takes off the hat that shades his face, pokes his finger into the hole his boss put in it with a shotgun during one late-night employee party, a dangerous trick the Frontier Town founder was known for.

"Think the bears will come?" Brandy asks.

"I know they'll come." His boss taps his temple. "I see it. And it happens. You're a seer too, I can tell. Probably that bit o' Cree in you. I think you know the answer to your question without me tellin' you."

The mechanical dog barks. The bears will come. He knows they will, just as he knows he has lost something besides his Ghost Wolf.

Stela

Her years in small-town Alabama brought three men in quick succession; Brian, Dustin, and Keenan. Huntsville, with its big spring and Civil War battlefield was the source of these three men she loved too much; who, in the end, gave her only their fleeting attentions, each relationship sidetracked by other women, or in the case of Keenan, a pulmonary edema at the age of 45. In their aftermath, Stela alone, her hands pulling at the vestiges of last year's tulips, emptying out the planting box, clearing the old growth to make way for the new. A fly tickles her ear and she swats it away with a wave of her wrist, thinking how long her curls have gotten and how a haircut might improve her mood.

Stela walks the rutted path to Christ the Scientist, a small wooden clapboard church on a side road across from the Winn Dixie. The puddles are dark brown with ice-melt, crushed by truck tires, shards of frost like broken glass on the ground. Vance charms her with his good manners and knowledge of Bible verses, and after clearing the plates and drying dishes together, he ventures to invite her to eat supper with him the next evening. Enough of men, she thinks, the words "No thank you" formed on her lips before they are replaced by "Yes," and the old, childhood need to please a man at any cost.

A fast courtship, the relationship devoid of any of the baggage and strife of her previous loves, Stela allows herself to believe in finally achieving a measure of happiness she'd once thought impossible. At night they sit on the porch of his A-frame house, listening to the radio and watching life unfold in the changing shape of the clouds.

The early summer nights on the porch, drinking scotch from crystal goblets, and teaching Vance about Gershwin and Schoenberg, the secondhand Victrola—bought to replace the one the Captain refused to let her have when she married— against the open window, always playing her music, give way to evenings at the Lions Club playing cards and sipping barrel-aged Bourbon. Stela accepts the new routine by making excuses for him, citing his exhausting work as a furniture upholsterer. A man has to have his time away, she thinks, the shadow of the Captain in front of her too faint for her to realize. She accepts the lessening of their love. To the strains of "Pierrot lunaire," she sings, "Skivvy. Cook. Cleaner. A fool, a fool, a fool." Her days weave into a seamless ribbon of frustration.

The holidays bring dreams of the Captain, how the idea of duty was bashed into her, the constant reminders, the harsh words, and the comfort of his arms in the aftermath of his rage. Vance, she thinks, is not my father; he's a good man worthy of my love, worthy of me accepting his shortcomings. Still, she never calls home, nor writes, save a card at Christmas.

Stone by stone, Vance buries Stela under a mound of insults. The belittling reduces her to a puddle of dishwater. Dinners become a means to gain favor, so she creates more and more elaborate meals. One Sunday night, a Duck *en Croute* in the oven, she phones the Lions Club to call him home. But he hasn't been seen there in weeks. "Cuckold. Cuckold," she hears the ridicule. In his desk drawer, beneath a sheaf of bills, she finds a phone number and name. Caroline Meagher: banjo lessons. The number is local. She dials and when the voice asks, "Hello? Who's there?" she hangs up, blushing.

Vance returns late evening. "How was the Lions Club?" she asks, searching his face for a hint. "Lost a bit, and I don't want to talk about it." He seats himself at the table and waits to be served. "What is this mess?" he asks. "It's vile." Buffeted by his words she rattles the dishes in the sink and chips a good plate. He's now in his chair reading the sports pages, ignorant of her.

Stela brushes her hair with her mother's silver brush and recalls the miserable life she'd led with the Captain. There's no need to gather any more evidence. The lie. The late-coming. The phone call. In bed her anger is mixed with elation, a sense of freedom. The knowledge that she can make a good plan to leave and that Vance won't know her intentions makes her smile.

At the library she discovers the banjo player lives in the next nearest town. There's a blurred picture of the woman in a news piece from the last Fourth of July Parade in that town. Hat tilted sideways, dimples, a banjo in her hands. She has the pinched look of an unhappy woman. Stela feels a pang of sadness, for she knows Vance will not find happiness there despite all his efforts. He is a ghost, searching for what cannot be found, for a love that does not exist.

Stela weaves a ribbon anew, of clear blue sky and towering aspen trees, birds swooping from branch to branch in a display of carefree ease. She longs to discover the single piece of thread that might signal the start of her next journey. On a Tuesday night, as she rubs a peppermint salve on her hands, she reads the lid. A cloud shaped like an angel, wings spread in flight, the print reads, "Vivalo. Las Cruces, NM."

That night her dreams are of adobe walls and blue-painted doors the color of the sky to keep the bad spirits at bay. She returns to the public library and the travel section. The house changes in small ways after her visit. A candle with the *Virgen de Guadelupe*. Rich-colored *ristretas*. A Georgia O'Keefe print of a cow's skull she finds at the thrift store. At night the cool breeze of escape suffuses their bedroom, Vance asleep, oblivious.

They sit down to a supper of stuffed bell peppers and wild rice. Vance is off to the Lions Club to "meet the boys." He kisses her on the cheek and drives away in the truck. Stela scrapes the leftovers into the trashcan and cleans the kitchen from top to bottom. She drags her small suitcase from under the bed in the spare room. She packed it the night she phoned the banjo player. In the living room she weeps for her loss. Her hand is warm on the wood of the Victrola. The precious records she can carry are in the suitcase, but leaving the record player is the worst abandonment of all.

She pays for her ticket, and as she pushes the bills across the counter her suitcase bursts open. She gathers her treasured objects, her talismans, and finds a seat in a darkened corner where she waits, $300 and a Greyhound ticket in her purse, for her bus to be called.

Las Cruces at night—red sky and the neon roadway signs of cheap motels. She rests her head on an unfamiliar pillow and sleeps a dreamless sleep, awakening to a frosty morning and the itch of freedom. At the reception desk she asks for directions to Vivalo. The clerk writes the path on a lined notepad and Stela pushes the double-door wide and strides into the sharp air of the New Mexican morning. On the telephone wires, crows sit spaced unevenly, yet Stela discerns a pattern in their spacing, musical notes that reorder themselves into the allegro of Copeland's "Appalachian Spring."

Brandy

He didn't know them right away; it was a year before he
began to even sense they were there—a cold draught, a
murmur, a sharp change in the air like nuggets being dropped
on metal scales.

After two years on the southern Montana prairie,
along the snaking Southern River with banks overwhelmed
with discarded rocks, a river that still yields gold dust, Brandy
knows for sure he isn't alone. The draughts become visions,
murmurs become voices, the changes in the air now carry
sound.

During the hours of 10 a.m. to 3 p.m., Monday
through Saturday, June through September, he's surrounded
by the living—like Prissy, who runs the front desk, selling
tickets to tourists passing by on Highway 1. Ageless, with a
gray-white bristly mustache, a biker boyfriend, and a sweet,
chirping voice, she reminds him of the frontierswomen who
settled Montana—she'd look just right in a bonnet and long
dress, swinging an ax to cut wood for the cook stove. She
doesn't care he is Cree, as some do.

Prissy mothers him in a gentle way he is not used to,
checks up on him during the long winter months. She
snowshoes over high drifts, bearing a stew or a goose thawed
and roasted from the fall hunt. "Hellooo," her voice rings
out, breaking winter's silence. "Glad you're still alive. Here's
some dinner. Should last you a week." He takes the enamel
kettle from her mittened hands and asks her in, desperate for
company. Her food isn't fancy, just good and hearty.

Like the earlier frontier town he'd worked in, this town was brought to life by one man, his new boss, Josh Whiteman, a local logger with a vision borne from peering through dust-encrusted panes of one of the few buildings still standing, facing the highway. Josh was surprised to see flowered Victorian wallpaper still intact, though dripping with water stains, and a puffy couch and matching chair. No one had looted in all these years. The idea came to Josh that people would pay money to see a real ghost town. Many abandoned pioneer homesteads and shanties littered the prairie. For the price of carting them over and laying them down, he could restore the original town plot.

Once the job was complete, Josh needed a full-time caretaker. Brandy saw the ad in the *Pennysaver* and applied. The day after he realized his wife was never coming back from girls' night out, Brandy filed for divorce and shook hands with Mr. Quigley, who then offered a bear hug and a small final bonus. Free room and board, away from all that reminded him of Elizabeth, and a chance to do what he loved best—building and repairing—was perfect.

He was given a log cabin, found nearby, built with more enthusiasm than materials by some rancher's grandfather. It faced the post office, saloon, other cabins, and one-room lean-tos. The schoolhouse steeple rose above them all, piercing the distant mountain range. "Do what you want to the inside, but leave the outside authentic," Josh instructed.

A new roof, coat of plaster, toilet behind a screen, a stove and refrigerator, his cousin's dreamcatcher over his cot, and he was home. Near the train tracks, he buried the items his wife had left behind.

When the town is filled with tourists and filmmakers, Brandy retreats to his cabin, away from the lookers poking and actors shooting blanks around the town he now considers his. He keeps curtains drawn against curious eyes, and naps or whittles. After the last tourist leaves he locks the entrance gates and makes sure all museum doors are closed to protect interiors from weather and animals. Sometimes Prissy follows him, sweeping dust and leaves that onlookers drag in. Prissy is the last person he sees, waving from the back of her boyfriend Zack's motorbike.

Still with daylight left, he roams the dirt streets and wooden boardwalks. Hops the acrylic barriers. Tries on hats, pokes around in old tobacco containers and pipes, continues the game of solitaire left unfinished on the saloon table. Takes his dinner of scrambled eggs or stew to the fancy house and eats at a mahogany table set for twelve, or to one of the cabins and eats at a wooden table set with a humble bread board and pewter pitcher. He grows accustomed to the old portrait photographs that watch him eating. Every sound is amplified—the crickets, the grouse beating its wings against the ground, the prairie wolf howling, his fork against the plate.

It is on one of those nights, eating dinner in the cabin next to his own, when he hears a noise behind him. It is a noise he can't place—he's grown so familiar with all of them. It sounds like silk against silk. He turns, but sees nothing in the evening's August melon light.

After that night, he hears more—footsteps, harnesses clanking—and he feels more—draughts, as if a door is opening, pushing air into the room.

He buys a hound and keeps it tethered up outside his cabin. This is no Ghost Wolf he is comfortable being haunted by.

After an uneventful winter, he welcomes the spring and the task of patching sod roofs. A dry summer follows. June, usually so wet, sees only sporadic rainfall. In July, when the sun beats down, punishing the grass and trees, he walks around the perimeter of the town looking and sniffing for the beginnings of brush fire. One day, dripping sweat all the way to the soles of his feet, finding himself a little faint, he sits under the post office's cool overhang. He watches young prairie dogs dart from hiding—from behind rocks, mounds, wagon wheels—to play in the road dust. A hawk circles overhead. A chipmunk found the peach pit he'd intentionally left on a boulder and turns it over in its small paws, examining. Silk rubs against silk.

He hears his name, whispered as softly as the silk sounded. It draws him to his feet, down the steps, down the main street to the schoolhouse, one of the original buildings that survived one hundred years of prairie weather. The front door is open like an invitation. Past wooden school desks, a teacher's podium, a silhouette of Lincoln, to the open doorway of the rear room. She lies on the schoolteacher's rope bed, in a white cotton shift, crying. He moves to comfort her instinctively, and she dissolves.

"Do you know anything about the schoolteacher who lived here?" he asks Josh.

Josh shrugs. "All we know is her name was Miz Annabelle Fourier, age twenty-two, French. She's on record for filing a complaint, charging two men in town with assault. Far as I can tell, charges were dropped. Why you wanna know?"

"I just want to get to know the place better."

To Brandy, the other ghosts remain sounds and stirrings only. Why only Annabelle shows herself, he doesn't know. Maybe he'd conjured her, maybe he'd brought her back from the dead the way his ancestors had hoped to bring back their slaughtered kin.

     After a few months of brief appearances she becomes ever present—in his cabin, in the haberdashery, in the tall grass by the low river. When her school bell rings out, the rope pulled by a tourist, the reverberations roll through him. She is not beautiful, his ghost, but he loves her freckled face, strong forearms, wispy red hair, and penetrating eyes that force him to care. They tie him to that place, those eyes, feed him and keep him steady. It is easy to love a ghost who asks nothing of you.

Stela

Snow blankets Las Cruces for a week. Stela visits Vivalo and buys another salve, this time blood-orange and vanilla, the fragrant citrus budding thoughts of spring and second chances in her heart. She wishes she'd been able to take the secondhand Victrola with her. The records sit in a box in her lodgings. Twice now in her life she's had to surrender her most cherished possession.

Work is as hard to find as green growth in the weeks Stela spends traipsing the slush-filled streets. On a gunmetal gray morning she loiters in the warmth of Vivalo, running her fingers along arrayed rows of greeting cards, chatting with Rosa, the owner, who keeps asking Stela how long she wants to stay in town.

"You know, when the thaw arrives and spring lands fully I could use some help here?" Rosa says.

"If I can last that long, I'd be grateful," Stela answers, turning a small statue of a coyote over in her hand.

A letter from Las Vegas waits for Stela when she gets back to her lodgings. Attorneys-at-Law: Rymer-Pardo-Unwin. The Captain is dead. Her mother, too. A car wreck outside Mobile. Late evening. Few details. Stela sinks to the ground and reads the rest of the page. She's executrix, whatever the hell that means? Estate sale, clear the mess of trucks, cars, old buildings.

Stela steadies herself at the old Victrola, and unsleeves Gershwin. The crackle of needle fizzes through her body and she sways to the slow rhythm. She lets her hand caress the wooden player, reunited with the object that was refused to her when she married Vance. Still, maybe the Captain kept it all these years for her. It wouldn't be like him to show sentiment, but she hums the music in her head and steers close to the coast of forgiveness, before veering away to the deeper waters of resentment again.

Brandy

Darkness always follows daylight. Daylight always follows darkness. Brandy, his foot on the wood stove, staring into the flaming belly. This is the season he dreads, deep winter. When days are filled with repetitive ticks and tocks and drips from leaky faucets and cracks and pops of burning wood. Snow so high the screen door won't open and he has to crawl out a window to get to the woodpile. Snow blind on a sunny day. Air so cold it sparkles. His breath a ream of hoar frost on his wool scarf. But at least he can move and wander. He rests under the sheltering evergreens, tracks deer troughs in the new powder. He doesn't need to hunt, that was done in the fall and he has plenty of carved, frozen meat in his freezer, but he needs to find something alive. There, brown hide, turned necks, then fleeing white tails and black hooves. On the way home, a screech in the sky, and he pauses to watch the hawk float on an unseen thermal. Brandy crawls back into his cabin, which smells, now that he has left it for a while and has breathed in clean air. Charred mutton, wood ash, kerosene, his own pungent scent on his clothes in the corner. He's back with himself, surrounded by himself. Even the ghosts that haunt the town he watches over keep to themselves in the cold. Museum shuttered up, the cattle gate entrance chained up, it's as if they are locked in their other worlds, not free to roam as when the tourist stop is open. Vapor, that's what some folks say they are, so maybe they freeze, too.

Brandy puts his foot up again on the stove, stares into the flame, and waits.

Sun paints his eyelids, skin, prairie winds whorl the dry grasses around him, and he is not alone. Annabelle lies beside him, silent as always, gazing up at the scudding clouds. For years now, this has been their joint habit and his comfort. When he rises to go back to work, she follows. He tramples the tall grass; she moves nothing in her wake.

He finishes his walk around the perimeter of the ghost town, looking for brush fire. It is a dry summer, and the Russian sage is catching in the nearby valleys. He can still see a dark smoke column rising in the west where a fire had burned for two days. The worst part about the tumbleweed is that it catches quickly and spreads easily when the wind picks up, as the bushes, some the size of small cars, let loose from the soil and do their dance of destruction far and wide.

It is also a chance to walk with Annabelle for a bit, her copper hair its own small fire on her head. He has aged, she has not, over the past decade he has been caretaking for the ghost town across from the Southern River, which is no longer a river really, more of a small stream during the rainier months. He has learned to value her silence. It means acceptance to him, pure and unadulterated acceptance of who he is. It leaves him with a solid core of peace inside.

But she will disappear when he gets back to the front of the museum where Prissy waits in the ticket booth, reading a Stephen King paperback. This day it is *Salem's Lot.* "Hey, Brandy, how you doin'? Slow day, here."

"Good. Nothing to report, area looks really dry but clear. Are you staying till three?"

"Yeah, the boss stopped by while you were out and told me he got a call from a whole busload of folks nearby looking for directions to the place, so I have to hold out till they get here and leave. At least we'll make some money today."

"OK, then, guess I'll retreat to my cabin."

Retreat is what Brandy does best. Remembering he has a sod roof to repair, he decides to wait till after three, when the place shuts its gates, to do his task.

His cabin up ahead, and there she is, waiting and looking out for him, her face distorted behind the old wavy glass.

They agree, standing by the charred ruins of the jailhouse, that the fire was probably started by one of the smoking tourists who had stamped out his or her cigarette on the wooden boardwalk out front. Brandy feels as if he'd had his head in his wood stove for hours, breathing in soot and smoke as he and his boss fought the flames that licked up the wooden structure. At the moment of throwing water on a nearby building to keep the fire from spreading, he recalled hearing somewhere how fire flickered up and in points due to its desire to flee gravity. That if a fire were to be set in space, it would stay in a round ball, like the sun.

Fire is as alive as the ghosts in this town, he thinks. He knows it is fighting for its life as they fight to smother it.

"We need to get some barrels with sand in it or something for smoking guests," Wilson tells Brandy. Exhausted, neither move for a long time. "And we need another jail."

The rough rumble of motorcycle exhaust, and Zack is pulling up with Prissy on the seat behind him. She jumps off, squeezes around the gatepost, yells as she approaches. "Hey! We saw the smoke from my house. Everyone OK?"

"Yeah," Wilson says. "We were lucky we cleared out the brush around all the buildings this spring. Fire didn't spread. Good work, Brandy."

Brandy recalls the hard days of pulling vines off walls and digging and spraying. If he hadn't done that just a couple of months ago, he might not have a job now. Or a place to live. Something he hides from, the fact that he has no place to be other than here.

Part II
July 24, 1982

Stela

With purpose, relentlessly back and forth, the broom sweeps the grass cuttings from the flags, her hips sway: an afternoon garden dance. The begonia by the door flushes an impatient hue, its energy sickle-scented mythic. In the sun she finds comfort in the wooden handle's rotation, the narrow lines ribbed a thousand times, hands grooved to a familiar shape. The bottle on the hall table migrates from the liquor cabinet all on its own—she has nothing to do with that, she'll later tell the guests. By then the cut blooms on the porch will have just the slightest wilt, the evening breeze blowing bed sheets on the washing line's threaded length. Perhaps she'll act like a character in a Tennessee Williams play, all sweaty and inviting in her wrapper dress, the one with the gardenia blossom printed in waves, cigarette smoking into closed air, Gershwin's "Rhapsody in Blue" on the gramophone. Perhaps.

Brandy

Eighteen crosses, one Madonna, one evergreen draped in tinsel. Brandy keeps track of the roadside shrines along I-70. He eventually pulls into his destination, an almost forgotten farmhouse, leaning a bit, scaling off its white paint, bed sheets billowing between two Tupelo trees. What he wants, what he was sent to save, is the old one-room jailhouse that waits, crouching in waist-high weeds near the front garden. What he expected to find was a driveway full of auction bidder's trucks and cars, spilling over onto the front lawn. His hand remains on the stick shift, his truck idling in the empty dirt drive. Perhaps he should leave, come back later. But someone in a mad-printed dress is waving to him from the porch, beckoning.

Stela

A line of mud stains the back of her stocking and with the palm of her hand she attempts to clean it off. *Don't go! Please.* The snap of the bed sheets in the wind startles the stranger in the truck, so she waves, not too desperately, she thinks. All she wants is to turn the brick jail to coin and buy her way out from this graveyard of the Captain's rusting trucks and cars. Run a hand along the dress, not too much, the colors an explosion of flowers. When he opens the door and clambers from the cab he is tall, tall, tall. "Hidy," he says, voice a box of unpolished stones from a dried-up riverbed. He smells of tobacco and a hint of clove. She drinks in the richness and squints her eyes so she can see him in sharper focus.

Brandy

He felt Annabelle's presence the whole way down. She whispered into his ear to mark each shrine they passed. Now, she is whipping the sheets in anger as he approaches this bright woman. A small swath in front of the house is mowed and the flagstones swept, a Mason jar with pink roses on a table by the front door she is framed by. Her palm is small and sweaty, callused from rough work. Welcomed inside, the pine floors rise up in odd places and a plant tendril wraps around a floor lamp and waves to him in the air. He takes off his Stetson. "My wisteria," she says, noticing his glance. "It's coming up through the floorboards and windowsills. I can't keep it at bay." She offers him a drink of lemonade or whiskey, and after they realize he is the only one coming to the auction, she calls the auctioneer to cancel and he accepts her lemonade. He pokes at the ice in the glass, fascinated by the sprigs of mint frozen into the cubes.

Stela

She pours the whiskey, amber into crystal, aware of his gray
eyes on the jail outside in the garden. "How much?" he asks,
his stare making her shiver, despite the humidity. "I'm paying
cash, remember." She names her price, adding a little for her
travel fund, the stack of the Captain's cash she found in the
open space inside the chimney. The light casts a shadow on
the wall behind him, and she thinks it's the wisteria and the
way it sways, almost a woman rocking in the wallpaper. He
says something she misses, one word. "Excuse me?" she says.
"Tart." He smiles, more lament than smile, the history of a
hard life captured in the lines grooved into his face. "The
lemonade." She nods, flicking a falling curl from her
forehead. She plucks at the elastic band holding her hair up,
and through half-closed lashes considers his arrival a rescue.
"Eureka. The lemons. The bitter kind," she says. Funny, she
thinks, how a ring of fine white light surrounds him as he
stands in front of the window. Stela feels an opening up
inside her, an expansion that is familiar, yet she cannot quite
determine its source.

Brandy

He is in another ghost town. Through the vine-covered window, rusty bodies of Fords and Chevys sprout milk thistle. Kudzu covers the frames in a green blanketing. The house in poorer condition than the refurbished ones in the Montana ghost town. Does she see ghosts, too? he wonders, turning to this woman, all color and warmth. She is looking at him in a way no living woman has looked at him in over a decade. He feels suddenly lost. Annabelle is just outside, pacing back and forth, unable to enter. Back and forth, like a metronome. Back and forth.

Stela

The room darkens, the clouds outside rolling black across the land, and the rattle of gardening tools suggests the wind is picking up. Yet, when she looks at the vine leaves, they are unmoving. More clamor from the porch and she goes to the door, but before she can open it, he steps toward her and places both hands on her shoulders. "You don't want to go out there." The heat from his fingers, the Gershwin's soothing notes, the thrum of rain on hard earth, she reaches toward his face.

Brandy

Tracing his jaw. Electrifying. Shoulders round and soft. The jail beckoning, his ghost screaming through the debris. Then abrupt silence. The needle glides off the etched vinyl after the final words ". . . spinning round." Brandy feels his face grow hot, steps back, fumbles for his wallet. It's all he has right now to give her, the wad of cash. He takes it out, fans it out, trying desperately to show her, it's all there.

Stela

She counts the bills. Recounts. Her fingers shake and notes flutter to the floor. She stoops to retrieve the money and at the same time he bends low to catch a falling bill. Their heads bump and a jolt of pain causes her to stand up, the bright sunlight sending sparks everywhere. He hands her the note, apologizing for the accident. His finger brushes her palm and she reddens, swallowing. Throat dry. "I need something to drink," she says, and moves to the Victrola where the pitcher of lemonade sits. Through blurred eyes she sees his approach, hands taking the pitcher and pouring. Her neck is hot, too hot. He hands her a glass and she puts it to her lips. She drinks. He drinks. His hand guides her to the sofa. The weight on his end sends her toward him.

Brandy

Brandy's arms take her in. She fell into them, almost thrown by the old dusty sofa with its broken springs. He freezes for a moment, startled. What to do? Breathes in the clean smell of mint and the heady scent of rosewater perfume. Whiskey and lemons on her breath. She won't push him away. Her blowsy hair, not in the feathered style so popular these days. It tickles his nose and he sneezes. This breaks the embrace and she jumps up, goes to the window. The wisteria waves at him from the corner, then seems to expand and reach for the woman framed by the window light, which is now expanding as clouds clear. Heat generated from panic builds in his torso as the vine nearly reaches a wrist. He grabs cutting shears from the end table and hacks at the greenery.

Stela

Stela wipes her brow with the sleeve of her dress, the moisture creating a dark smear on the fabric. The metallic clack of the shears rings in her ears and she collapses back onto the sofa, overcome. When the cutting stops she opens her eyes and he is in front of her. There's a look in his eyes she cannot quite decipher; not desire or passion, rather a fearful look, she thinks. The shears dangle from his hand and the blades are stained from his frantic activity. She reaches out for his hand to pull him down. He coughs, then moves to the half-full glass on the Victrola. The record sleeve falls to the floor and Stela reaches for it at the same time as he does. "Please." It is all she can say.

Brandy

Brandy knows there is no other way in to the house for
Annabelle, that the haint blue paint he'd noticed on the porch
ceiling when he'd walked under it is keeping her out, except
in this one way. He is angry with himself. It is as if he severed
her arm when he cut through the vine. He just wants to get
the deal done and leave, ride back to his cabin and hide out
with his silent ghost. This one is already asking for more than
he can give, he can tell. And why so soon? He knows he is
not a handsome man, just passable these days, and is not even
shaven after the long drive. Can smell his body odor, getting
stronger by the minute. As she replaces the record sleeve on
the turntable, he smells something else, something acrid at
the edge of his nostrils. Fire. Trained to look out for it, he
knows in an instant. "She's burning you out!" he cries,
grabbing the woman and running for the door, the shears still
in his clenched hand.

Stela

Acrid. Her eyes stinging, Stela falls out the door, down the
steps, and stumbles onto the dry ground. Brandy drops the
shears and kneels by her, the shadow of the porch darkening
his face. Another shadow tracks across the hard earth of the
yard, moving away from the house. The look on Brandy's
face is a mix of anguish and confusion. "Where's the fire?"
she asks. He wipes both hands on his shirt and shakes his
head. "No fire. Only the memory of one." He cradles Stela's
head to keep her hair off the ground. She notices large paw
prints in the dirt dust, too large to be a local stray's prints.
After a minute's quiet he helps her to her feet. "Is it safe to
go back inside?" she asks. He nods, taking her arm and
guiding her to the door. As he crosses the threshold once
more, Stela feels Brandy's grip weaken on her arm.

Brandy

"Stay," Stela says. One word. So loaded. She lays her hand, which is fluttering like a breeze-tossed leaf, on his arm once again. It burns but is gentle. Brandy looks to the shadow of Annabelle retreating, and a smaller one chasing, growing fainter, two gray masses disappearing between the blades of grass, the stems of vines. This new woman's scent, her wanting eyes, bluff manner, soft skin, her quirky hair and house, causes his stiff knees to settle on the canted floorboards. He knows something without knowing it, looks up at Stela and says, "For how long?"

The Authors Wish to Thank . . .

Jamez Chang, hip-hop artist, poet, and editor, who originally solicited a flash collaboration for *Counterexample Poetics*. That story, "Eighteen Crosses, One Madonna," received much attention and gave us the idea to expand it. Thank you, Jamez, for your contribution to flash in general and for your support of our work!

Conium Press, who gave *The Bitter Kind* semifinalist status in their chapbook contest.

Gloria Mindock, publisher of Červená Barva Press, for loving this little novelette and helping to bring it into the world and for being such a supportive, wonderful soul. The lit world would not be the same without Gloria and Bill.

Ashley Inguanta, for the use of her stunning cover photograph. No other image would have sufficed. We thank her for the gift of her art and friendship.

Arun Padykula, for adjusting the image to make it even more moody.

Sophie Appel, cover designer, for taking the photo and doing something very special with it, as always.

Lori Hettler, our wonderful PR person who helped spread the word.

ALL of our blurbers, Mel Bosworth, Kathy Fish, Kimberly Lojewski, Michael Martone, and Robert Scotellaro, for their time, kind words, and their own writing contributions that have inspired us. We're in awe of each one of you.

And each other:

James Claffey, my partner in crime, one of my favorite authors and human beings. Thank you for working with me, riffing off my prose, and making this a fun, rewarding project. I couldn't wait to open my email to see what Stela was doing next! It was an honor.

Tara Masih, astounding collaborator and friend. Thank you for sharing this process, the collaboration, the inventiveness, the strangeness of these two characters. Also, for all your hard work and diligence bringing our project to publication, thank you.

And you:

The reader. Thank you for taking part in our collaborative experiment. By your act of reading, you are now the third collaborator in the room.

Note: Stela appeared in James Claffey's *Blood a Cold Blue* (Press 53) as part of "Gardenia & Tarot"; Brandy appeared in Tara Lynn Masih's *Where the Dog Star Never Glows* (Press 53) in "Ghost Dance." Big thanks as well to Press 53 publisher Kevin Watson for his early support of our writing.

Author Biographies

Tara Lynn Masih is editor of *The Rose Metal Press Field Guide to Writing Flash Fiction* and *The Chalk Circle* (both Foreword Books of the Year), author of *Where the Dog Star Never Glows*, and Founding Series Editor of *The Best Small Fictions*. Her flash has been heavily anthologized in such collections as *Brevity & Echo; Flashed: Sudden Stories in Comics and Prose; Nothing Short of 100;* and in W.W. Norton's *New Micro: Exceptionally Short Fiction*. *My Real Name Is Hanna*, her debut novel, was a National Jewish Book Awards Finalist and winner of a Julia Ward Howe Award.

James Claffey grew up in Dublin, Ireland, and currently lives in California. His collection of short fiction, *Blood a Cold Blue*, is published by Press 53. He is currently putting the finishing edits to a novel set in 1980s Dublin. His short fiction piece "Skull of a Sheep," which first appeared in the *New Orleans Review*, is in W.W. Norton's *Flash Fiction International*. His flash fiction "Kingmaker," which first appeared in *Five Points: A Journal of Literature and Art*, also features in W.W. Norton's *New Micro: Exceptionally Short Fiction*. "The Third Time My Father Tried to Kill Me" was published in *The Best Small Fictions 2015*, and he was a finalist in *The Best Small Fictions 2016*. His work has appeared in numerous journals and magazines, and when not writing he teaches high school English in Santa Barbara.